A GATHERING OF
GHOST STORIES

ROBERTSON DAVIES

A GATHERING OF
GHOST STORIES

penguin books

PENGUIN BOOKS
Published by the Penguin Group
Penguin Books USA Inc., 375 Hudson Street,
New York, New York 10014, U.S.A.
Penguin Books Ltd, 27 Wrights Lane,
London W8 5TZ, England
Penguin Books Australia Ltd, Ringwood,
Victoria, Australia
Penguin Books Canada Ltd, 10 Alcorn Avenue,
Toronto, Ontario, Canada M4V 3B2
Penguin Books (N.Z.) Ltd, 182–190 Wairau Road,
Auckland 10, New Zealand

Penguin Books Ltd, Registered Offices:
Harmondsworth, Middlesex, England

Published in Penguin Books 1995

The six selections in this book appear in Mr. Davies's *High Spirits*,
published by Penguin Books.

ISBN 0 14 60.0112 5

Printed in the United States of America

CONTENTS

A GATHERING OF
GHOST STORIES

How the High Spirits Came About

A CHAPTER OF AUTOBIOGRAPHY

Ghost stories came into my life before I could read. How well I remember the first one; it was at a party given by my parents, and it was not yet time for me to go to bed, because I remember that the sun was sinking outside the windows, and as the guests ate tulip jellies—they were streaked red and yellow and topped with whipped cream of a deliciousness that seems to have departed from the earth—Mrs. Currie told the strange tale of the Disappearance of Oliver Lurch. He was a farm youth in Kentucky who had gone out one night from a gathering just like ours, to fetch some wood for the fire, had not returned and when the others went to seek him he could be heard calling from the sky, 'Here I am! Here I am! Help me! I am Oliver Lurch!' The cries became fainter and fainter, and Oliver was heard and seen no more. There were those who said he had been carried off by a great eagle but—a grown man? What sort of eagle was that? It must have been Something Else.

I fell asleep that night fearing the Mighty Clutch. And since then I have always felt that any party would be the better for a ghost story.

The first uncanny tale I read, when I was ten, was *Frankenstein*, which terrified me unforgettably and gloriously. None of the film versions, in my opinion, comes near the effect Mary Shelley produces by her special quality of prose. A story in this collection, *The Cat That Went to Trinity*, obviously owes much to this favourite of mine, and although it is far from serious, it is not meant to be derisive of the great original. No disrespect toward serious spectres is intended herein.

Although I have read tales of ghosts and the supernatural eagerly all my life I never thought of writing one until I went to Massey College in the University of Toronto, in 1963. The college had a Christmas party for its members and their friends, and some sort of entertainment was needed. There were lots of gifted people to call on— poets and musicians—but I was expected to make a contribution, and I decided on a ghost story, the one which appears first in this book. For the eighteen years I was at the college a story was called for every Christmas, and here they are, gathered together, in the hope that other enthusiasts for this sort of tale will enjoy them.

It was never my intention to frighten anyone. Indeed I do not think that would have been possible; the audience was too big and to me, at least, terror is best when the group of listeners is small. No, these stories were to amuse, and perhaps to add a dimension to a building and 2 a community that was brand-new. University College has a ghost, of which it is justifiably proud, and doubtless there are others around the University which have not yet found their chroniclers. Massey College is a building of great architectural beauty, and few things become architecture so well as a whiff of the past, and a hint of the uncanny. Canada needs ghosts, as a dietary supplement, a vitamin taken to stave off that most dreadful of modern ailments, the Rational Rickets.

Let no one suppose that I was the first to think that a few hauntings might be acceptable in the new college. Very early in its first autumn I was told that a figure had taken to appearing on the stairs, and in dark corners, who frightened some people, and disappeared when bolder people pursued it. I have never thought of myself as a ghost-catcher, but my work at the college demanded some unusual tasks, and I accepted this one as part of the job. I captured the ghost at last—sneaked up on him from behind—and he proved to be one of the students who, with a sheet and an ugly rubber mask, was trying to cheer the place up. That was his explanation, but there was a gleam in his eye that suggested to me that the ghost game fulfilled some need in his own character. That was not hard to understand, for he was engaged in a particularly rational and hard-headed form of study, and too much rationality, as I have suggested, calls for a balancing element.

Writing ghost stories, and in particular, cheerful ghost

stories, set me to the task of examining the literature of the ghost story, and its technique. There are some very famous ghost stories, and perhaps the acknowledged masterpiece is Henry James' *The Turn of the Screw*. James casts it in the form of a tale read at Christmas time to a party of friends in an English country house; what could be better? It is without doubt the best of James' substantial and distinguished contribution to this branch of literature. There are also the fine stories written by Montague Rhodes James, which he composed and at first read aloud to groups of friends at King's, Cambridge, and later at Eton, where he was Provost. My father-in-law heard him on a few of these occasions and many years later described to me the special pleasure they gave. Parties of friends, college occasions: yes, we could provide these elements at the Massey College Gaudy Nights; the word comes from the Latin *gaude*, and has long been applied to college parties. But what about style?

Ghost stories tend to be very serious affairs. Who has ever heard of a ghost cracking a joke? I wanted my ghosts to be light-hearted, if not in themselves, at least as they appeared to my hearers. No new style would suit a ghost story, so it would be necessary to parody the usual style. And the parody would have to be affectionate, for cruel parody is distasteful in itself, and utterly outside the spirit of a party.

4   I think I know the traditional ghost story style pretty

thoroughly. It is solemn, and it frequently makes use of unusual words, designed to strike awe into the minds of the reader or the hearer. It is a style that can very easily become ridiculous, and even such a great master of the ghost story as Joseph Sheridan LeFanu does not always escape this peril. Poor LeFanu not only wrote uncanny tales, he lived one. The story has been told many times that he suffered from a recurrent nightmare, in which he stood at the foot of a macabre and menacing house which towered high in the air, and which he knew was about to collapse on him. When he died in 1873, of a heart seizure, his physician remarked dryly that the house had fallen at last.

It is one of the regrets of my life that I missed seeing, and perhaps even having some conversations with, a man who was a great scholar in the realm of magic, uncanny happenings, and of course ghost stories. He was, to give him his full resounding title and name, the Reverend Father Alphonsus Joseph-Mary Augustus Montague Summers, chiefly known for his work in the realm of Restoration drama, but also the author of *The History of Witchcraft* and many other books about werewolves, Satanism and the supernatural. He was a rum customer. He had left his home in Oxford shortly before I went there in 1936 and was remembered with affection, some mirth, and now and then with unexpected venom. He appeared in the streets dressed like a European priest, in cassock and shovel-hat, with a cloak and a bulky umbrella; some stories insisted that he always walked in the gutter, for no determinable reason. But—and it was this that raised eyebrows—he was invariably accompanied on his afternoon walk *either* by a pallid youth dressed in black, who was supposed to be his secretary, *or* by a large black dog, but never by both! Tongues wagged.

Although I never met Father Summers, I have all my life collected his books, among which are several collections of ghost stories, some of which he wrote himself, and to all of which he appends learned discussions of the kind of literature he knew and loved so well. His prose style, which sets the teeth of more austere readers on edge, fills me with delight. He had read so many tales of the supernatural, pored over so many old manuscripts and *grimoires*, that his writing had been infected by them, and displays a fruit cakyness and portwinyness that makes for very rich literary feeding. He delights in words like 'sepulture' and 'charnel' which it would be a pity to allow to fall out of the language. So when I set to work to write some ghost stories, with a glint of parody in my eye, I determined also to lay a few laurels on the tomb of that not always wholly admired scholar, Montague Summers. I shall be pleased if those who know his work feel that I have not altogether failed.

My ghosts are sufficiently traditional, in that they all
appear in search of something. This is the usual reason

for ghostly appearances; something has been lost, or some revenge or justice is sought, and the spirit cannot rest until this unfinished business is concluded. If that is established, it is obvious that the proper greeting to a ghost is not a shriek of terror but a courteous 'What can I do for you?' It was Shelley who wrote—and I echo him—

> While yet a boy I sought for ghosts, and sped
>   Through many a listening chamber, cave and ruin,
>   And starlit wood, with fearful steps pursuing
> Hopes of high talk with the departed dead.

In my ghost stories I have tried to explore where such high talk might lead.

Anybody who writes ghost stories is sure to be asked: do you believe in ghosts? And the answer to that must be, I believe in them precisely as Shakespeare believed in them. People who want further discussion may be referred to that model of good sense, Dr. Samuel Johnson, who said:

> It is wonderful that five thousand years have now elapsed since the creation of the world, and still it is undecided whether or not there has ever been an instance of the spirit of any person appearing after death. All argument is against it, but all belief is for it.

All belief? The Doctor speaks with his accustomed certainty. Much belief, undoubtedly, for in 1954–55 the popular Swiss fortnightly *Schweizerischer Beobachter* published a series of articles on prophetic dreams, coincidences, premonitions and ghosts, and then asked readers who had any experience of such things to write to the Editor. The response was overwhelming; more than 1200 readers wrote in, giving more than 1500 cases of personal experience; and these writers were people of education and discretion. It is interesting that most of the letter-writers confided their names to the Editor but asked that they be not made public; few people will admit to all the world that they believe in the supernatural. These letters were confided by the paper to the late Dr. C. G. Jung, whose secretary, Mrs. Aniela Jaffe, published them with psychological comment, and extremely interesting reading they make. So it may be said that if not everybody believes in ghosts, there are a great many people who certainly do not disbelieve in them.

One word remains to be said: I have not edited these stories specifically for the reader; they remain in the form in which they were first spoken aloud, and I beg you— you readers—to grant them the attention of the ear, as well as of the eye. Perhaps, as in my case, your first ghost story was *heard*.

The names of several living people, associated in one way or another with Massey College, appear in these stories. Never, let me say, are they mentioned in anything except an affectionate and genial spirit, as befits a Gaudy Night, and I hope that the bearers of these names will not feel that I have been impudently free with them, or suggested an acceptance of the supernatural which they may disclaim. These are, after all, party-ghosts, emanating from high spirits.

Revelation from a Smoky Fire

At the outset of a personal ghost story, it is accepted practice to say that one is the least fanciful person in the world, that one has not a nerve in one's body, doesn't believe in ghosts, and can't understand how it happened. I am therefore at a disadvantage, for I am a more than ordinarily fanciful person, I am extremely nervous, I don't find anything intrinsically improbable in the notion of a ghost, and I have a pretty shrewd idea how it happened. Therefore I am more likely to distress myself than to alarm you by what I am going to recount; I know that in the ghost controversy you are all overwhelmingly of the anti-ghost party. But I can assure you that I found it a disquieting experience.

The fire in my study smokes. It is not merely that the Bursar buys green wood; something is amiss with the chimney. Sometimes it smokes so much that I feel like those Jesuit missionaries who used to fling themselves on the floor in the longhouses of the Canadian Indians, because only within six inches of the floor could one breathe the air without tearing the lungs.

10   My fire was smoking yesterday afternoon at dusk, as I

sat reading the précis of an M.A. thesis. My nerves would have been quieter had I been reading a ghost story; thesis abstracts are, with a very few exceptions, the least credible and most horrifying productions of imaginative literature. Nevertheless you will understand that I was not in the least disposed to see a ghost, though I was rather far advanced in asphyxiation.

At last, reluctantly, like a man approaching a task he knows to be outside human power, I went to the fire and knelt to poke it, thinking perhaps I might alter the quality of the smoke, and thus secure change, if not relief. Of course I simply made it worse. I grew impatient, and holding my breath, put my head into the worst of the smother, to see if anything—a bird's nest, or a dead squirrel, or anything of that sort, might have stuck in the chimney.

Nothing. Defeated, and with the disgruntled resignation of one used to such defeats, I crawled backward into the room, and stood up.

There was a man sitting at my desk.

Nothing in the least alarming about that. People quite often come into my study without being heard; when I am busy I often do not notice what is happening around me. I assumed he was a visitor. He looked like a senior faculty member—a tall, rather lean, bald man, with professorial eyebrows. He was wearing his gown, but so was I, for that matter for, though smoky, my study was cold.

'Good afternoon,' I said; 'can I help you?'

'You can help me by doing something about that smoking chimney,' he replied.

He smiled as he spoke, and I assumed that this was some form of donnish humour. Nevertheless, I thought it rather cool of him to complain about what was, after all, *my* chimney. I decided to take the line of extreme and disarming courtesy, which sometimes works well with impudent people.

'I assure you I am doing the best I can,' said I.

'Not a very good best,' said he; 'take another look up the flue.'

I obeyed. Not, you understand, because I was awed by him, but because I wanted time to think. Slowly I knelt, and poked my head into the fireplace again, and thought.

Who the devil is he? There is something familiar about his face, but what is his name? I wish I could either forget both faces and names, or remember both. It is this perpetual dealing with nameless faces that makes my life a muddle of uncertainty. Is he one of those architectural critics who still push their way into the college, and take on airs? How dare he give me orders? I *must* have met him somewhere. Is he one of those dons who suffers from the delusion that he is Dr. Johnson, and is rude on principle?

By this time I had thought all I could, without drawing in huge breaths of smoke, so I crawled back into the room and stood up again.

'If I were you I'd go up on the roof and put a rod down that chimney,' said the stranger. 'Or why don't you come down it again?'

'Down the chimney?' said I. Aha, this was the clue. Here was a madman.

'Yes,' said he; 'you didn't knock at the door, so I assume you must have come down the chimney. You weren't here a minute ago.'

One of my cardinal rules in life is always to humour madmen. It is second nature to me. I do it several times every day.

'Quite so,' said I. 'I came down the chimney.'

He looked at me closely, and I thought somewhat insultingly.

'Tight squeeze, wasn't it?' said he.

'Not in the least,' I replied. 'A chimney with a good clear draught might be a little swift for a man of my age and quiet habit of life, but this is a superbly smoky chimney—and the smoke, as you readily understand, gives just that density to the atmosphere in the flue which permits me to float down as gently as a feather. Science, you observe,' I said this airily, for I was beginning to enjoy myself.

'Look here,' said he; 'I don't believe you're a chimney sweep at all.'

'Your perception is in perfect order,' said I. 'I am not

a chimney sweep; I am the Master of this College. Now may I ask who you are?'

'Aha,' he cried, 'just as I thought. You're a madman. I don't believe in humouring madmen. Out you go!'

'As you please,' said I. He looked as though he might become violent, and I wanted time to edge myself toward the bell which calls the Porter. 'But before I go, would you have the goodness to tell me who you are?'

'I?' he shouted, working the tremendous eyebrows in a way which I could tell had been effective in quelling undergraduates. 'Certainly I'll tell you. *I* am Master of this College.'

'Of course,' said I, in my silkiest tones, 'but which Master are you?'

'Damn your impudence,' he roared, 'I'm the ninth Master.'

I confess this made me feel very unwell. I can't tell why, but it did, and although I cannot fully describe the sensation, I thought I was going to faint; for a time my consciousness seemed to come and go in rhythmic waves; it was like vertigo, only more intense; I was horribly distressed. But my visitor seemed even more so.

'Stop! Stop!' he cried; 'for God's sake don't fade and reappear like that. You make me giddy.' And to my astonishment he fell back into my chair and closed his eyes, as white as—well, as white as a ghost. I forgot all about the
Porter, and hurried to his side. I put out my hand to feel

his brow, just as he opened his eyes. I was amazed to see unmistakable fear in his face, and he shrank from my touch.

'Don't be afraid,' I said, 'I only want to help you.' His voice was faint, and came from a dry mouth. 'Who did you say you were?' he asked.

'I am the first Master,' said I. Presumably I was distressed more than I realized, for though I was trying to reassure him my voice sounded sad and eerie, even to myself.

'Then you are—Finch?' he said.

Again the inexplicable malaise overcame me, and I could tell by the fear in his eyes that, to his vision, I must be fading and reappearing again. My sensations were mingled; to be mistaken for Robert Finch—painter, poet, musician, scholar, wit and distinguished diner-out— presented me with an extreme of temptation. Should I risk all, and bask for a moment in another's glory? But decency prevailed. I denied, reluctantly, that I was Finch.

'Good God! then—you must be the other fellow who was here, briefly, even before Finch,' said he.

Condemn me, if you will, as an egotist, but in such a situation which of you could have contained his curiosity? 'What became of him—that other fellow who was here, briefly, before Finch?' I asked. And again I heard in my own voice that hollow, eerie note.

He shook his head. 'I don't really know,' he said; 'it was

whispered that something happened that occasionally happened to professors in those days; something called "making a composition with his creditors", or some quaint phrase of the kind, and he went.'

'Where did he go?' I persisted. The man looked as if he needed fresh air, but the subject was of such importance to me that I put my own interest first.

'I don't think anybody knew,' he said. 'The story that has come down to us is that there was a full-dress enquiry in the Round Room, and it is presumed that the Visitor broke the Master, for when it was over he stumbled out into the quad, and it was seen that the russet rosette had been torn from his gown. After that—well, some said it was the pool, and some said he leapt from the tower, and some said'—here his voice thickened with repugnance—'that he went off and got a job at York. The College behaved very well toward the wife and girls; they kept going by taking in washing for some of the Junior Fellows who couldn't afford the Coin Wash. Finch was a man of very delicate feeling, by all accounts, and he saw to it. But it was all so long ago. . .'

My concern for his suffering had considerably abated. Madman he might be, but. . .'How long ago?' I asked.

'A century, at least,' said he. 'Let's see—this is Christmas, 2063—oh, yes; a full century.'

'A century, and nine Masters?' said I. And again that

dreadful sensation, like going down too rapidly in an elevator.

'A distinguished group,' said he, with complacency, 'Let's see—before me—I'm in my fourth year now—there was Kasabowszki for twenty-one years, poor Sawyers who died after three, Taschereau who made it for ten, Gamble for twelve, Meyer for seven, Duruset for fifteen, poor Polanyi—worn out with waiting, really,—for three, and of course Finch's glorious first mastership of twenty-five long, sunny years. Yes, nine Masters from the beginning.'

I knew I was dealing with a madman. I knew that I was behaving foolishly, but I couldn't help myself. 'Nine, you idiot!' I shouted. 'Ten, ten, ten! I was first Master—' I stopped, shocked at what I had said, and hurried to change the dreadful word. 'I *am* first Master,' I screamed.

I suppose I must have looked dreadful, waving my arms and shouting, for he shrank back into my chair, and covered his face with his hands. But I could hear him muttering.

'It isn't true,' he was whispering to himself. 'Reason and science—everything I have lived by—are against it. I'm not seeing a ghost. I utterly deny that I am seeing a ghost.'

These words affected me dreadfully. I felt as though every fibre and bone of my body were melting into something insubstantial, and my control of myself deserted me utterly. 'Ghost!' I screamed; 'ghost yourself! Ghost your- 17 self!' But even as I protested a fearful sickness of doubt was mounting to my heart. I needed help, not for the madman in my chair but for myself. I pushed the bell for the Porter; that way lay sanity; an old army man would know what to do.

The Porter came faster than I could have hoped—but what a Porter! Six feet four of ex-naval man, a bo'sun if ever I saw one. He went at once to the figure in my chair.

'I heard you shouting, sir,' said he; 'anything I can do?'

'Get rid of that—thing there by the fireplace,' said the impostor, pointing toward me, but keeping his eyes closed.

'Nothing there, sir,' said the Porter. 'Better let me help you out into the air, sir. Terrible smoky fire you have to-day.'

Nothing there! The words struck me like a heavy blow and I swooned.

How long it was I do not know, but some time later I was aroused to find Mr. McCracken helping me to my feet.

'Better let me help you out into the air, sir,' he said. 'Terrible smoky fire you have today.'

'Yes,' I said; 'we must ask the Bursar for some seasoned wood.'

The Ghost Who Vanished by Degrees

Some of you may have wondered what became of our College Ghost. Because we had a ghost, and there are people in this room who saw him. He appeared briefly last year at the College Dance on the stairs up to this Hall, and at the Gaudy he was seen to come and go through that door, while I was reading an account of another strange experience of mine. I did not see him then, but several people did so. What became of him?

I know. I am responsible for his disappearance. I think I may say without unwarrantable spiritual pride that I laid him. And, as is always the case in these psychic experiences, it was not without great cost to myself.

When first the ghost was reported to me, I assumed that we had a practical joker within the College. Yet—the nature of the joke was against any such conclusion. We had had plenty of jokes—socks in the pool, fish in the pool, funny notices beside the pool, pumpkins on the roofs, ringing the bell at strange hours—all the wild exuberance, the bubbling, ungovernable high spirits and gossamer fantasy one associates with the Graduate School of the University of Toronto. The wit of a graduate student is like champagne—Canadian champagne—but this joke had a different flavour, a dash of wormwood, in its nature.

You see, the ghost was so unlike a joker. He did not appear in a white sheet and shout 'Boo!' He spoke to no one, though a Junior Fellow—the one who met him on the stairs—told me that the Ghost passed him, softly laying a finger on its lips to caution him to silence. On its lips, did I say? Now this is of first importance: it laid its finger where its lips doubtless were, but its lips could not be seen, nor any of its features. Everybody who saw it said that the Ghost had a head, and a place where its face ought to be—but no face that anybody could see or recognize or remember. Of course there are scores of people like that around the university, but they are not silent; they are clamouring to establish some sort of identity; the Ghost cherished his anonymity, his facelessness. So, perversely I determined to find out who he was.

The first time I spotted him was in the Common Room. I went in from my Study after midnight to turn out the lights, and he was just to be seen going along the short passage to the Upper Library. I gave chase, but when I reached the Upper Library he had gone, and when I ran into the entry, he was not to be seen. But at last I was on his trail, and I kept my eyes open from that time.

All of this took place, you should know, last Christmas, between the Gaudy and New Year. Our Gaudy last year was on December the seventeenth; I first saw the Ghost,

20

and lost him, on the twenty-first. He came again on the twenty-third. I woke in the night with an odd sensation that someone was watching me, and as this was in my own bedroom I was very angry; if indeed it were a joker he lacked all discretion. I heard a stirring and—I know this sounds like the shabbiest kind of nineteenth century romance, but I swear it is true—I heard a sigh, and then on the landing outside my door, a soft explosion, and a thud, as though something had fallen. I ran out of my room, but there was nothing to be seen. Over Christmas Day and Boxing Day I had no news of the Ghost, but on the twenty-eighth of December matters came to a head.

December the twenty-eighth, as some of you may know, is the Feast of the Holy Innocents, traditionally the day on which King Herod slaughtered the children of Bethlehem. In the Italian shops in this city you can buy very pretty little babies, made of sugar, and eat them, in grisly commemoration of Herod's whimsical act.

I was sitting in my study at about eleven o'clock that night, reflectively nibbling at the head of a sugarbaby and thinking about money, when I noticed that the lights were on in the Round Room. It troubles me to see electric current wasted, so I set out for the Round Room in a bad humour. As I walked across the quad, it seemed that the glow from the skylight in the Round Room was more blue and cold than it should be, and seemed to waver. I thought it must be a trick of the snow, which was falling softly, and the moonlight which played so prettily upon it.

I unlocked the doors, walked into the Round Room, and there he was, standing under the middle of the sky-light. He bowed courteously. 'So you have come at last,' said he.

'I have come to turn out the lights,' said I, and realized at once that the lights were not on. The room glowed with a fitful bluish light, not disagreeable but inexpressibly sad. And the stranger spoke in a voice which was sad, yet beautiful.

It was his voice which first told me who he was. It had a compelling, 'cello-like note which was unlike anything I was accustomed to hear inside the College, though our range is from the dispirited quack of Ontario to the reverberant splendours of Nigeria. The magnificent voice came from the part of his head where a face should be—but there was no face there, only a shadow, which seemed to change a little in density as I looked at it. It was unquestionably the Ghost!

This was no joker, no disguised Junior Fellow. He was our Ghost, and like every proper ghost he was transporting and other-worldly, rather than merely alarming. I felt no fear as I looked at him, but I was deeply uneasy.

'You have come at last,' said the Ghost. 'I have waited for you long—but of course you are busy. Every professor 22 in this university is busy. He is talking, or he is pursuing, or he is in a journey, or peradventure he sleepeth. But none has time for an act of mercy.'

It pleased me to hear the Ghost quote Scripture; if we must have apparitions, by all means let them be literate.

'You have come here for mercy?' said I.

'I have come for the ordeal, which is also the ultimate mercy,' he replied.

'But we don't go in for ordeals,' said I. 'Perhaps you can tell me a little more plainly what it is you want?'

'Is this not the Graduate School?' said he.

'No indeed,' said I; 'this is a graduate college, but the offices of the Graduate School are elsewhere.'

'Don't trifle with me,' said the Ghost sternly. 'Many things are growing very dim to me, but I have not wholly lost my sense of place; this is the Graduate School; this is the Examination Room. And yet'—the voice faltered—'it seemed to me that it used to be much higher in the air, much less handsome than this. I remember stairs—very many stairs . . .'

'You had been climbing stairs when you came to me in my bedroom' and I.

'Yes,' he said eagerly. 'I climbed the stairs—right to the top—and went into the Examination room—and there you lay in bed, and I knew I had missed it again. And so there was nothing for it but to kill myself again.'

That settled it. Now I knew who he was, and I had a 23

pretty shrewd idea where, so far as he was concerned, we both were.

Every university has its secrets—things which are nobody's fault, but which are open to serious misunderstanding. Thirty or more years ago a graduate student was ploughed on his Ph.D. oral; he must have expected something of the kind because when he had been called before his examiners and given the bad news he stepped out on the landing and shot himself through the head. It is said, whether truly or not I cannot tell, that since that time nobody is allowed to proceed to the presentation and defence of his thesis unless there is a probability amounting to a certainty that he will get his degree.

Here, obviously, was that unfortunate young man, standing with me in the Round Room. Why here? Because, before Massey College was built, the Graduate School was housed in an old dwelling on this land, and the Examination Room was at the top of the house, as nearly as possible where my bedroom is now. Before that time the place had been the home of one of the Greek-letter fraternities—the Mu Kau Mu, I believe it was called.

'The Examination Room you knew has gone,' said I. 'If you are looking for it, I fear you must go to Teperman's wrecking yard, for whatever remains of it is there.'

'But is this not an Examination Room?' said the Ghost. I nodded. 'Then I beg you, by all that is merciful, to examine me,' he cried, and to my embarrassed astonishment, threw himself at my feet.

'Examine you for what?' I said.

'For my Ph.D.', wailed the Ghost, and the eerie, agonized tone in which it uttered those commonplace letters made me, for the first time, afraid. 'I must have it. I knew no rest when I was in the world of men, because I was seeking it; I know no rest now, as I linger on the threshold of another life, because I lack it. I shall never be at peace without it.'

I have often heard it said that the Ph.D. is a vastly overvalued degree, but I had not previously thought that it might stand between a man and his eternal rest. I was becoming as agitated as the Ghost.

'My good creature,' said I, rather emotionally, 'if I can be of any assistance—'

'You can,' cried the Ghost, clawing at the knees of my trousers with its transparent hands; 'examine me, I beg of you. Examine me now and set me free. I'm quite ready.'

'But, just a moment,' said I; 'the papers—the copies of your thesis—'

'All ready,' said the Ghost, in triumph. And, though I swear that they were not there before, I now saw that all the circle of tables in the Round Room was piled high with those dismal, unappetizing volumes—great wads of typewritten octavo paper—which are Ph.D. theses.

'Be reasonable,' said I. 'I don't suppose for a minute I can examine you. What is your field?'

'What's yours?' said the Ghost, and if a Ghost can speak cunningly, that is exactly what this one did now.

'English literature,' I said; 'more precisely, the drama of the nineteenth century, with special emphasis on the popular drama of the transpontine London theatres between 1800 and 1850.'

Most people find that discouraging, and change the subject. But the Ghost positively frisked to one of the heaps, drew out an especially thick thesis, and handed it to me.

'Shall I sit here?' he asked, pointing to the red chair, which, as you know, has a place of special prominence in that room.

'By no means,' said I, shocked by such an idea.

'Oh, I had so hoped I might,' said the Ghost.

'My dear fellow, you have been listening to University gossip,' said I. 'There are people who pretend that we put the examinee in that chair and sit around the room in a ring, baiting him till he bursts into tears. It is the sort of legend in which scientists and other mythomaniacs take delight. No, no; if you will go away for a few hours—say until tomorrow at ten o'clock—I shall have the room set up for an examination. You shall have a soft chair, cheek by jowl with your examiners, with lots of cigarettes, unlimited water to drink, a fan, and a trained nurse in attendance to take you to the Examinees' W.C. and bring you back again, should the need occur. We are very well aware here that Ph.D. candidates are delicate creatures, subject to unaccountable metaphysical ills—'

The Ghost broke in, impatiently. 'Rubbish,' he said; 'I'm quite ready. Let's get to work. You sit in the red chair. I'm perfectly happy to stand. I think I'm pretty well prepared'—and as he said this I swear that something like a leer passed over the shadow that should have been a face—'and I'm ready as soon as you are.'

There was nothing for it. The Ghost had taken command. I sat down in the red chair—my chair—and opened the thesis. *Prologomena to the Study of the Christ Symbol in the Plays of Thomas Egerton Wilks,* I read, and my heart, which had been sinking for the last few moments now plunged so suddenly that I almost lost consciousness. I have heard of Wilks—it is my job to have heard of him—but of his fifty-odd melodramas, farces and burlesque extravaganzas I have not read a line. However, I have my modest store of professor-craft. I opened the thesis, riffled through the pages, hummed and hawed a little, made a small mark in the margin of one page, and said—'Well, suppose for a beginning, you give me a general outline of your argument.'

He did.

Forty-five minutes later, when I could get a word in, I asked him just where he thought the Christ symbol made its first appearance in *My Wife's Dentist*, or *The Balcony Beau* which is one of Wilks' dreary farces.

He told me.

Before he had finished he had also given me more knowledge than I really wanted about the Christ symbol in *Woman's Love or Kate Wynsley the Cottage Girl*, *Raffaelle the Reprobate, or the Secret Mission and the Signet Ring*, *The Ruby Ring, or The Murder at Sadlers Wells*, and another farce named, more simply, *Bamboozling*.

By this time I felt that I had been sufficiently bamboozled myself, so I asked him to retire, while the examination board—me, me, and only me, as the old song puts it—considered his case. When I was alone I sought to calm myself with a drink of water, and after a decent interval I called him back.

'There are a few minor errors in this thesis which you will undoubtedly notice during a calm re-reading, and a certain opaqueness of style which might profitably be amended. I am surprised that you have made so little use of the great Variorum Edition of Wilks published by Professors Fawcett and Pale, of the University of Bitter End, Idaho. Nevertheless I find it to be a piece of research of real, if limited value, which, if published, might be—yes, I shall go so far as to say, will be—seminal in the field of nineteenth century drama studies,' said I. 'I congratulate you, and it will be a pleasure to recommend that you receive your degree.'

I don't know what I expected then. Perhaps I hoped that he would disappear, with a seraphic smile. True enough, there was an atmosphere as of a smile, but it was the smile of a giant refreshed. 'Good,' he said; 'now we can get on to my other subjects.'

'Do you mean to say that nineteenth century drama isn't your real subject?' I cried, and when I say 'I cried,' I really mean it; my voice came out in a loud, horrified croak.

'Sir,' said he; 'it is so long ago since my unfortunate experience at my first examination that I have utterly forgotten what my subject was. But I have had time since then to prepare myself for any eventuality. I have written theses on everything. Shall we go on now to History?'

I was too astonished, and horrified, and by this time afraid, to say anything. We went on to History.

My knowledge of History is that of a layman. Academically, there is nothing worse, of course, that can be said. But professor-craft did not wholly desert me. The first principle, when you don't know anything about the subject of a thesis, is to let the candidate talk, nodding now and then with an ambiguous smile. He thinks you know, and are counting his mistakes, and it unnerves him. The Ghost was an excellent examinee; that is to say, he fell for it, and I think I shook his confidence once with a little laugh, when he was talking about Canada's encouragement of the arts under the premiership of W. L. Mackenzie King. But finally the two hours was up, and I graciously gave him his Ph.D. in History.

Next came classics. His thesis was on *The Concept of Pure Existence in Plotinus*. You don't want to hear about it, but I must pause long enough to say that I scored rather heavily by my application of the second principle of conducting an oral, which is to pretend ignorance, and ask for explanations of very simple points. Of course your ignorance is real, but the examinee thinks you are being subtle, and that he is making an ass of himself, and this rattles him.

And so, laboriously, we toiled through the Liberal Arts, and some of the Arts which are not so liberal. I examined him in Computer Science, and Astronomy, and Mediaeval Studies, and I rather enjoyed examining him in Fine Art. One of my best examinations was in Mathematics, though personally my knowledge stops short at the twelve-times table.

Every examination took two hours, but my watch did not record them. The night seemed endless. As it wore on I remembered that at cockcrow all ghosts must disappear, and I cudgelled my brain trying to remember whether the kosher butchers on Spadina keep live cocks, and if so what chance we had of hearing one in the Round Room. I was wilting under my ordeal, but the Ghost was as fresh as a daisy.

30   'Science, now!' he positively shouted, as a whole new

mountain of theses appeared from—I suppose from Hell. Now I know nothing whatever of Science, in any of its forms. If Sir Charles Snow wants a prime example of the ignorant Arts man, who has not even heard of that wretched law of thermodynamics, which is supposed to be as fine as Shakespeare, he is at liberty to make free with my name. I don't know and I don't care. When the Ghost moved into Science I thought my reason would desert me.

I needn't have worried. The Ghost was as full of himself as a Ghost can possible be, and he hectored and bullied and badgered me about things I had never heard of, while my head swam. But little by little—it was when the Ghost was chattering animatedly about his work on the rate of decay of cosmic rays when they are brought in contact with mesons—that I realized the truth. The Ghost did not care whether I knew what he was talking about or not. The Ghost was a typical examinee, and he wanted two things and two things only—an ear into which he could pour what he believed to be unique and valuable knowledge, and a licence to go elsewhere and pour it into the ears of students. Once I grasped this principle, my spirits rose. I began to nod, to smile, to murmur appreciatively. When the Ghost said something especially spirited about the meiosis-function in the formation of germ-cells, I even allowed myself to say 'Bravo'—as if he had come upon something splendid that I had always suspected myself but had never had time to prove in my lab- 31 oratory. It was a great success; I knew that dawn could not be far away, for as each examination was passed, the Ghost seemed to become a little less substantial. I could see through him, now, and I was happily confident that he could not, and never would, see through me. As he completed his last defense of a doctoral dissertation, I was moved to be generous.

'A distinguished showing,' I said. 'With a candidate of such unusual versatility I am tempted to go a little beyond the usual congratulations. Is there anything else you fancy—a Diploma in Public Health, for instance, or perhaps something advanced in Household Science?'

But the Ghost shook his head. 'I want a Ph.D. and that only,' said he. 'I want a Ph.D. in everything.'

'Consider it yours,' said I.

'You mean that I may present myself at the next Convocation?'

'Yes; when the Registrar kneels to take upon him the degrees granted to those who are forced by circumstances to be absent, I suggest that you momentarily invest him with your ectoplasm—or whatever it is that people in your situation do,' said I.

'I shall; Oh, I shall,' he cried, ecstatically, and as he faded before my eyes I heard his voice from above the skylight in the Round Room, saying, 'I go to a better place than this, confident that as a Ph.D. I shall have it in 32 my power to make it better still.'

So at last, as dawn stole over the College, I was alone in the Round Room. The night of the Holy Innocents had passed. Musing, my hand stole to my pocket and, pulling out the sugarbaby, I crunched off its head. Was it those blessed children, I wondered, who had hovered over me, protecting me from being found out? Or had it perhaps been the spirit of King Herod, notoriously the patron of examiners?

All things considered, I think it was both great spiritual forces, watching over me during the long night. Happy in the thought that I was so variously protected, I stepped out into the first light, the last crumbs of the sugarbaby still sweet upon my lips.

The Cat That Went to Trinity

Every Autumn when I meet my new classes, I look them over to see if there are any pretty girls in them. This is not a custom peculiar to me: all professors do it: I also count the number of young men who are wearing Chairman Mao coats, or horseshoe moustaches. A pretty girl is something on which I can rest my eyes with pleasure while another student is reading a carefully-researched but uninspiring paper.

This year, in my seminar on the Gothic Novel, there was an exceptionally pretty girl, whose name was Elizabeth Lavenza. I thought it a coincidence that this should also be the name of the heroine of one of the novels we were about to study—no less a work than Mary Shelley's celebrated romance *Frankenstein*. When I mentioned it to her she brushed it aside as of no significance.

'I was born in Geneva,' said she, 'where lots of people are called Lavenza.'

Nevertheless, it lingered in my mind, and I mentioned it to one of my colleagues, who is a celebrated literary critic.

34 'You have coincidence on the brain,' he said. 'Ever

since you wrote that book—*Fourth Dimension* or whatever it was called—you've talked about nothing else. Forget it.'

I tried, but I couldn't forget it. It troubled me even more after I had met the new group of Junior Fellows in this College, for one of them was young Einstein, who was studying Medical Biophysics. He was a brilliant young man, who came to us with glowing recommendations; some mention was made of a great-uncle of his, an Albert Einstein, whose name meant nothing to me, though it appeared to have special significance in the scientific world. It was young Mr. Einstein's given names that roused an echo in my consciousness, for he was called Victor Frank.

For those among you who have not been reading Gothic Novels lately, I may explain that in Mrs. Shelley's book *Frankenstein, or The Modern Prometheus*, the hero's name is also Victor, and the girl he loved was Elizabeth Lavenza. This richness of coincidence might trouble a mind less disposed to such reflection than mine. I held my peace, for I had been cowed by what my friend the literary critic had said. But I was dogged by apprehension, for I know the disposition of the atmosphere of Massey College to constellate extraordinary elements. Thus, cowed and dogged, I kept my eyes open for what might happen.

It was no more than a matter of days when Fate added another figure to this coincidental pattern, and Fate's instrument was none other than my wife. It is our custom to entertain the men of the College to dinner, in small groups, and my wife invites a few girls to each of these occasions to lighten what might otherwise be a too exclusively academic atmosphere. The night that Frank Einstein appeared in our drawing room he maintained his usual reserved—not to say morose—demeanour until Elizabeth Lavenza entered the room. Their meeting was, in one sense, a melodramatic cliché. But we must remember that things become clichés because they are of frequent occurrence, and powerful impact. Everything fell out as a thoroughly bad writer might describe it. Their eyes met across the room. His glance was electric; hers ecstatic. The rest of the company seemed to part before them as he moved to her side. He never left it all evening. She had eyes for no other. From time to time his eyes rose in ardour, while hers fell in modest transport. This rising and falling of eyes was so portentously and swooningly apparent that one or two of our senior guests felt positively unwell, as though aboard ship. My heart sank. My wife's on the contrary, was uplifted. As I passed her during the serving of the meal I hissed, 'This is Fate.' 'There is no armour against Fate,' she hissed in return. It is a combination of words not easily hissed, but she hissed it.

We had an unusually fine Autumn, as you will recall, and there was hardly a day that I did not see Frank and

Elizabeth sitting on one of the benches in the quad, sometimes talking, but usually looking deep into each other's eyes, their foreheads touching. They did it so much that they both became slightly cross-eyed, and my dismay mounted. I determined if humanly possible to avert some disastrous outcome (for I assure you that my intuition and my knowledge of the curious atmosphere of this College both oppressed me with boding) and I did all that lay in my power. I heaped work on Elizabeth Lavenza; I demanded the ultimate from her in reading of the Gothic novel, both as a means of keeping her from Frank, and straightening her vision.

Alas, how puny are our best efforts to avert a foreordained event! One day I saw Frank in the quad, sitting on the bench alone, reading a book. Pretending nonchalance, I sat beside him. 'And what are you reading, Mr. Einstein?' I said in honeyed tones.

Taciturn as always, he held out the book for me to see. It was *Frankenstein*. 'Liz said I ought to read it,' he said.

'And what do you make of it?' said I, for I am always interested in the puny efforts of art to penetrate the thoroughly scientific mind. His answer astonished me.

'Not bad at all,' said he. 'The Medical Biophysics aspect of the plot is very old-fashioned, of course. I mean when the hero makes that synthetic human being out of scraps from slaughter-houses. We could do better than that now. A lot better,' he added, and I thought he seemed 37 to be brooding on nameless possibilities. I decided to change the line of our conversation. I began to talk about the College, and some of the successes and failures we had met with in the past.

Among the failures I mentioned our inability to keep a College Cat. In the ten years of our existence we have had several cats here, but not one of them has remained with us. They all run away, and there is strong evidence that they all go to Trinity. I thought at one time that they must be Anglican cats, and they objected to our oecumenical chapel. I went to the length of getting a Persian cat, raised in the Zoroastrian faith, but it only lasted two days. There is a fine Persian rug in Trinity Chapel. Our most recent cat had been christened Episcopuss, in the hope that this thoroughly Anglican title would content it; furthermore, the Lionel Massey Fund provided money to treat the cat to a surgical operation which is generally thought to lift a cat's mind above purely sectarian considerations. But it, too, left us for Trinity. Rationalists in the College suggested that Trinity has more, and richer, garbage than we have, but I still believe our cats acted on religious impulse.

As I spoke of these things Frank Einstein became more animated than I had ever known him. 'I get it,' he said; 'you want a cat that has been specifically programmed for Massey. An oecumenical cat, highly intelligent so that it prefers graduates to undergraduates, and incapable of making messes in the Round Room. With a few hours of computer time it oughtn't to be too difficult.'

I looked into his eyes—though from a greater distance than was usual to Elizabeth Lavenza—and what I saw there caused a familiar shudder to convulse my entire being. It is the shudder I feel when I know, for a certainty, that Massey College is about to be the scene of yet another macabre event.

Nevertheless, in the pressure of examinations and lectures, I forgot my uneasiness, and might perhaps have dismissed the matter from my mind if two further interrelated circumstances—I dare not use the word coincidence in this case—had not aroused my fears again. One autumn morning, reading *The Globe and Mail*, my eye was caught by an item, almost lost at the bottom of a column, which bore the heading 'Outrage at Pound'; it appeared that two masked bandits, a man and a woman, had held up the keeper of the pound at gunpoint, while seizing no less than twelve stray cats. Later that same day I saw Frank and Elizabeth coming through the College gate, carrying a large and heavy sack. From the sack dripped a substance which I recognized, with horror, as blood. I picked up a little of it on the tip of my finger; a hasty corpuscle count confirmed my suspicion that the blood was not human.

Night after night in the weeks that followed, I crept down to my study to look across the quad and see if a light was burning in Frank Einstein's room. Invariably it was so. And one morning, when I had wakened early and was standing on my balcony, apostrophizing the dawn, Elizabeth Lavenza stole past me from the College's main gate, her face marked, not by those lineaments of slaked desire so common among our visitors at such an hour, but by the pallor and fatigue of one well-nigh exhausted by intellectual work of the most demanding sort.

The following night I awoke from sleep at around two o'clock with a terrifying apprehension that something was happening in the College which I should investigate. Shouts, the sound of loud music, the riot of late revellers—these things do not particularly disturb me, but there is a quality of deep silence which I know to be the accompaniment of evil. Wearily and reluctantly I rose, wrapped myself in a heavy dressing-gown and made my way into the quadrangle and there—yes, it was as I had feared—the eerie gleam from Frank Einstein's room was the only light to guide me. For there was a thick fog hanging over the University, and even the cruel light through the arrow-slits of the Robarts Library, and the faery radiance from OISE were hidden.

Up to his room I climbed, and tapped on the door. It had not been locked, and my light knock caused it to swing open and there—never can I forget my shock and 40 revulsion at what I saw!—there were Frank and Elizabeth crouched over a table upon which lay an ensanguined form. I burst upon them.

'What bloody feast is this?' I shouted. 'Monsters, fiends, cannibals, what do I behold?'

'Shhh,' said Elizabeth; 'Frank's busy.'

'I'm making your cat,' said Frank.

'Cat,' I shrieked, almost beside myself; 'that is no cat. It's as big as a donkey. What cat are you talking about?'

'The Massey College cat,' said Frank. 'And it is going to be the greatest cat you have ever seen.'

I shall not trouble you with a detailed report of the conversation that followed. What emerged was this: Frank, beneath the uncommunicative exterior of a scientist, had a kindly heart, and he had been touched by the unlucky history of Massey College and its cats. 'What you said was,' said he to me, 'that the College never seemed to get the right cat. To you, with your simple, emotional, literary approach to the problem, this was an insuperable difficulty: to my finely-organized biophysical sensibility, it was simply a matter of discovering what kind of cat was wanted, and producing it. Not by the outmoded method of selective breeding, but by the direct creation of the Ideal College Cat, or ICC as I came to think of it. Do you remember that when you talked to me about it I was reading that crazy book Liz was studying with you, about the fellow who made a man? Do you remember what he said? "Whence did the principle of life proceed? It was a bold question, and one which has ever been considered as a mystery; yet with how many things are we upon the brink of becoming acquainted, if cowardice or carelessness did not restrain our enquiries". That was written in 1818. Since then the principle of life has become quite well known, but most scientists are afraid to work on the knowledge they have. You remember that the fellow in the book decided to make a man, but he found the work too fiddly if he made a man of ordinary size, so he decided to make a giant. Me too. A cat of ordinary size is a nuisance, so I decided to multiply the dimensions by twelve. And like the fellow in the book I got my materials and went to work. Here is your cat, about three-quarters finished.'

The fatal weakness, the tragic flaw in my character is foolish good-nature, and that, combined with an uninformed but lively scientific curiosity led me into what was, I now perceive, a terrible mistake. I was so interested in what Frank was doing that I allowed him to go ahead, and instead of sleeping at nights I crept up to his room, where Frank and Elizabeth allowed me, after I had given my promise not to interfere or touch anything, to sit in a corner and watch them. Those weeks were perhaps the most intensely lived that I have ever known. Beneath my eyes the ICC grew and took form. By day the carcass was kept in the freezer at Rochdale, where Elizabeth had a room; each night Frank warmed it up and set to work.

The ICC had many novel features which distinguished

it from the ordinary domestic cat. Not only was it as big as twelve ordinary cats; it had twelve times the musculature. Frank said proudly that when it was finished it would be able to jump right over the College buildings. Another of its beauties was that it possessed a novel means of elimination. The trouble with all cats is that they seem to be housebroken, but in moments of stress or laziness they relapse into an intolerable bohemianism which creates problems for the cleaning staff. In a twelve-power cat this could be a serious defect. But Frank's cat was made with a small shovel on the end of its tail with which it could, once a week, remove its own ashes and deposit them behind the College in the parking-space occupied by *The Varsity*, where, it was assumed, they would never be noticed. I must hasten to add that the cat was made to sustain itself on a diet of waste-paper, of which we have plenty, and that what it produced in the manner I have described was not unlike confetti.

But the special beauty of the ICC was that it could talk. This, in the minds of Frank and Elizabeth, was its great feature as a College pet. Instead of mewing monotonously when stroked, it would be able to enter into conversation with the College men, and as we pride ourselves on being a community of scholars, it was to be provided with a class of conversation, and a vocabulary, infinitely superior to that of, for instance, a parrot.

This was Elizabeth's special care, and because she was

by this time deep in my course on the Gothic Novel she decided, as a compliment to me, to so program the cat that it would speak in the language appropriate to that *genre* of literature. I was not so confident about this refinement as were Frank and Elizabeth, for I knew more about Gothic Novels than they, and have sometimes admitted to myself that they can be wordy. But as I have told you, I was a party to this great adventure only in the character of a spectator, and I was not to interfere. So I held my peace, hoping that the cat would, in the fulness of time, do the same.

At last the great night came, when the cat was to be invested with life. I sat in my corner, my eyes fixed upon the form which Frank was gradually melting out with Elizabeth's electric hair-dryer. It was a sight to strike awe into the boldest heart.

I never dared to make my doubts about the great experiment known to Frank and Elizabeth, but I may tell you that my misgivings were many and acute. I am a creature of my time in that I fully understand that persons of merely aesthetic bias and training, like myself, should be silent in the presence of men of science, who know best about everything. But it was plain to me that the ICC was hideous. Not only was it the size of twelve cats, but the skins of twelve cats had been made to serve as its outer envelope. Four of these cats had been black, four were white, and four were of a marmalade colour. Frank, who liked things to be orderly, had arranged them so that the cat was piebald in mathematically exact squares. Because no ordinary cat's eyes would fit into the huge skull the eyes of a goat had been obtained—I dared not ask how— and as everyone knows, a goat's eyes are flat and have an uncanny oblong pupil. The teeth had been secured at a bargain rate from a denturist, and as I looked at them I knew why dentists say that these people must be kept in check. The tail, with the shovel at the end of it, was disagreeably naked. Its whiskers were like knitting needles. Indeed, the whole appearance of the cat was monstrous and diabolical. In the most exact sense of the words, it was the damnedest thing you ever saw. But Frank had a mind above appearances and to Elizabeth, so beautiful herself, whatever Frank did was right.

The moment had arrived when this marvel of science was to be set going. I know that Frank was entirely scientific, but to my old-fashioned eye he looked like an alchemist as, with his dressing-gown floating around him, he began to read formulae out of a notebook, and Elizabeth worked switches and levers at his command. Suddenly there was a flash, of lightning it seemed to me, and I knew that we had launched the ICC upon its great adventure.

'Come here and look,' said Frank. I crept forward, half-afraid yet half-elated that I should be witness to such a triumph of medical biophysics. I leaned over the frightful creature, restraining my revulsion. Slowly, dreamily, the goat's eyes opened and focussed upon me.

'My Creator!' screamed the cat in a very loud voice, that agreed perfectly with the hideousness of its outward person. 'A thousand, thousand blessings be upon Thee. Hallowed be Thy name! Thy kingdom come! O rapture, rapture thus to behold the golden dawn!' With which words the cat leapt upon an electric lamp and ate the bulb.

To say that I recoiled is to trifle with words. I leapt backward into a chair and cringed against the wall. The cat pursued me, shrieking Gothic praise and endearment. It put out its monstrous tongue and licked my hand. Imagine, if you can, the tongue of a cat which is twelve cats rolled into one. It was weeks before the skin-graft made necessary by this single caress was completed. But I am ahead of my story.

'No, no,' I cried; 'my dear animal, listen to reason. I am not your Creator. Not in the least. You owe this precious gift of life to my young friend here.'

I waved my bleeding hand toward Frank. In their rapture he and Elizabeth were locked in a close embrace. That did it. Horrid, fiendish jealousy swept through the cat's whole being. All its twelve coats stood on end, the goat's eyes glared with fury, and its shovel tail lashed like that of a tiger. It sprang at Elizabeth, and with a single

stroke of its powerful forepaws flung her to the ground.

I am proud to think that in that terrible moment I remembered what to do. I have always loved circuses, and I know that no trainer of tigers ever approaches his beasts without a chair in his hand. I seized up a chair and, in the approved manner drove the monstrous creature into a corner. But what I said was not in tune with my action, or the high drama of the moment. I admit it frankly; my words were inadequate.

'You mustn't harm Miss Lavenza,' I said, primly; 'she is Mr. Einstein's fiancée.'

But Frank's words—or rather his single word—were even more inadequate than my own. 'Scat!' he shouted, kneeling by the bleeding form of his fainting beloved.

Elizabeth was to blame for programming that cat with a vocabulary culled from the Gothic Novel. 'Oh, Frankenstein,' it yowled, in that tremendous voice; 'be not equitable to every other and trample upon me alone, to whom thy justice and even thy clemency and affection is most due. Remember that I am thy creature; I ought to be thy Adam; dub me not rather the fallen angel, whom thou drivest hence only because I love—nay reverence thee. Jealousy of thy love makes me a fiend. Make me happy, and I shall once more be virtuous.'

There is something about that kind of talk that influences everybody that hears it. I was astonished to hear Frank—who was generally contented with the utilitarian vocabulary of the scientific man—say—'Begone! I will not 47 hear you. There can be no community between thee and me; we are enemies. Cursed be the day, abhorred devil, in which you first saw the light! You have left me no power to consider whether I am just to you or not. Begone! Relieve me of the sight of your detested form!'

Elizabeth was not the most gifted of my students, and the cat's next words lacked something of the true Gothic rhetoric. 'You mean you don't love your own dear little Pussikins best,' it whined. But Frank was true to the Gothic vein. 'This lady is the mistress of my affections, and I acknowledge no Pussikins before her,' he cried.

The cat was suddenly a picture of desolation, of rejection, of love denied. Its vocabulary moved back into high gear. 'Thus I relieve thee, my creator. Thus I take from thee a sight which you abhor. Farewell!' And with one gigantic bound it leapt through the window into the quadrangle, and I heard the thundrous sound as the College gate was torn from its hinges.

I know where it went, and I felt deeply sorry for Trinity.

The King Enjoys His Own Again

A hundred and fifty years is a long time, you will all
agree, for a man to suffer misunderstanding and wrong.
My task tonight is to attempt to put right such a misunderstanding. The length of time I have mentioned makes
it clear at once that I am speaking on behalf of a ghost.
Oh, if it were only one ghost! Because there are two; and
I can feel them very near me as I address you now. Both
are determined that I should support the version of the
history of this University that they think the right one.
Much hangs on which side I take.

A week ago tonight we held our College Christmas
Dance. My wife and I left at about one o'clock, and went
to bed, but I was unable to sleep. I had an uneasy sense
that someone had been there whom I had failed to greet,
because I try to speak, or at least leer hospitably, at everybody. I rose: I prowled. I went to a window and, looking
down, I was surprised to see someone in the quadrangle
walking alone in a posture of dejection—someone in an
academic gown.

Gowns are often seen in the quad, but—at two in the
morning? And was there not about the figure a singular-

ity, a distinction greater than is common among academics? I went out into the night for a nearer look.

Whoever it was paced up and down the stone paths, and as I came nearer, I heard what was unquestionably the sound of deep sobs. The figure was weeping! Some unhappy youth who had been, as they say, given the mitt by his partner at the dance? I hid behind a tree, to hear better. The broken utterance became audible: 'O, the black ingratitude of it,' said the rich, fruity voice; 'All this fuss, and not a word—not one solitary word—about me. It's cruel, cruel!' I am not a man to withhold sympathy from any suffering soul, and I popped out from behind my tree.

'Excuse me,' said I; 'may I be of any assistance—' At that moment the figure moved into a gleam of moonlight, and you may judge of my dismay when I saw that the moonlight passed right through it! A cold greater than that of December seized upon me and my heart sank. For I knew that this much-haunted establishment was once again being visited by a ghost. But whose ghost this time?

Then I knew. It could be none other. What I had mistaken for a gown was in fact a voluminous cloak, and when the figure turned to me the elegance of the clothes beneath the ghostly yet blinding blaze of stars and orders and diamonds in the moonlight, and more than anything else that great head, that florid, fleshy face, that beaky nose, those drooping eyelids, and the splendidly curled chestnut hair could belong to but one person. It was King George the Fourth. I bowed. It is not easy to bow elegantly in pyjamas, but old theatrical training came to my aid and I think it was not a bad bow. 'Your Majesty,' said I.

'So you know me,' said the figure. 'I had concluded that I was utterly forgotten here.'

I muttered something about the University Department of History.

'Pah,' said the King. 'Deluded toadies to a totally wrong principle. I should know. I *am* History, suppressed and distorted History. O Ingratitude! How sharper than a serpent's tooth it is to have founded a thankless University.' I mumbled some disclaimer, but the King spoke on. 'It is now 1977 and this graceless institution is celebrating what it is pleased to call its Sesquicentennial. But has a word been said about the Monarch who, by a stroke of the pen, brought it into being? Don't think I'm angry. No, no. But I am hurt. Deeply, terribly hurt. So what have you to say?'

Me? It is not my job to deal with such things. Let the Public Relations people explain. Let the President explain. Let the Lieutenant-Governor, who acted as Chairman of the Sesquicentennial Committee, explain. But none of them were there. No, no; they were snug in their beds, and I was face to face with a sobbing, ignored Founder.

'I can only appeal to your magnanimity, Sire,' I said. 'You know what academics are. Simple folk whose minds rarely stray beyond the present. And really, I—what can I do?'

'I'll tell you in good time,' said the King. 'But first a matter of curiosity; something led me here; something led me to this place; some notion that in this College, at least, I might find understanding. What do you think it can have been?'

What was I to say? 'Humble as I am,' I ventured, 'I apologize on behalf of us all. I am sure no affront was intended.'

He was not mollified. A look of bitterness succeeded to grief in his countenance. 'Pshaw,' he said. 'I notice none of you forgot John Strachan. Tell me, what does this University find that is so special about John Strachan?'

I spoke without thinking, 'As our Founder—' said I, causing the King to interrupt in a temper.

'Oh Founder, Founder, Founder! Strachan was forever founding something! McGill University, your great rival— he had a finger in that pie. And Trinity, your neighbour—they toady to him there as a Founder. But in this University he wasn't a Founder, he was merely an organizer! Did he ever open his sporran and lay down a penny-piece? Because I did! This University would have been nowhere without my money.'

The word 'money' as we all know, has strong magical

overtones. Silently, but impressively, we were joined by another figure, and to my experienced eye that figure was a phantom. It was John Strachan, without a doubt, in the full day-dress of an Anglican Bishop—gaiters, apron, squarecut long coat, and above all that peculiar hat like a stovepipe with a wireless aerial on either side, which gives a Bishop the appearance of one who is in perpetual receipt of messages from outer space. His square, granite face was marked with the look of intense disapproval so often seen in the Scot who has risen high in the world. John Strachan, without a doubt. The word 'money' had brought him back from the grave.

'Did I hear a suggestion,' he said in a withering tone, 'That I contributed nothing to the founding of this institution?'

'No money, at any rate,' said the King, who had no fear of this apparition. 'I laid down a sturdy thousand pounds a year, which in terms of today's money was very handsome. Indeed, I can't understand, with what must be a hundred and fifty thousand pounds of my money, why this place is in need of money now.'

'As I recall, that money was provided from public funds,' said the Bishop.

But the King did not bat an eye. 'I suppose it was,' said he; 'I could hardly be expected to fuss about where it *came* from. The important fact is that I *granted* it and you *got* it, so I suppose we may say you had it from me.'

'Your Majesty might say that,' said the Bishop, 'but other donors have given from their own pockets.'

'Meaning yourself, I suppose?' said the King.

'A Bishop does not make known his contributions to worthy causes,' said John Strachan.

'That's gammon,' said the King. 'Come along, Strachan, how much real money did you stump up?'

'I must respectfully request your Majesty not to press a question that offends against Christian principle,' said the Bishop, and I thought he seemed uncomfortable.

'Aha! Got you,' said the King; 'I'll wager fifty guineas you gave nothing at all,' and he laughed like a schoolboy.

'Sir, you are disrespectful of my cloth,' shouted Strachan, fire darting from his eyes.

'Pish for your cloth,' said the King. 'Your cloth may be well enough, but the cut and fit are abominable. If you mean I don't respect you as a Bishop, you're wrong. It is well-known that I was vastly respectful of Bishops, when I chose my own. But you were one of my niece Victoria's creations, and she had a sentimental taste for Scotchmen.'

Now it was the Bishop's turn to show hurt feelings. Tears dimmed those stony eyes. 'This is a man's reward for a life of the most stringent devotion to God, to duty and the cause of education,' said he; 'how sharper than a serpent's tooth it is to meet a thankless Monarch!'

'Fiddle-faddle,' said the King. 'What do you need of 54 gratitude from your Monarch. Your name has been whooped and hallooed about this University for the past year, and more. You've had more gratitude than you deserve, because much of it was filched from me!'

The Bishop stopped weeping, and roared. 'You! Who slaved and contrived to set this University firmly on its feet? Who endured the reproach and ignominy of an ungrateful government and an indifferent populace? Whose hair turned gray under the strain of that shocking and discriminatory Charter you signed—without reading it, I am sure—until I was able to enlarge its scope and make a University that was truly for the people of this great land?'

'A University which you subsequently described as 'a godless imitation of Babel,' said the King; 'and after you had given it that nasty dig you skipped away and founded Trinity, which was much more to your liking. Oh, you were a mighty Founder, and such a tyrant as no King would dare to emulate. Don't lecture me as if I didn't know this University's history. Don't I remember (after my time on earth, of course) when the greedy Government took it over as an addition to their lunatic asylum, and didn't they have the ugliness to call it the University Lunatic Asylum? Not such a bad name, when you think of it. And don't twaddle about your hair going gray. No man needs to endure such things if he has a good valet.' And here King George IV touched his head with conscious pride, and indeed his splendidly curled wig was a work of art.

'Huuut!' said the Bishop. It was his version of a laugh. 'Vanity of vanities, all is vanity.'

'That's one of the truest things in the Bible,' said the King, quite affably. 'If it weren't for vanity we should still be running about in our skins, painted a horrid blue. Vanity is one of the mainsprings of human progress.'

The King seemed to be getting the better of the argument. I remembered that John Strachan's motto had been *Prudent But Fearless.* Now he showed a sudden change of mood toward what, in a character less granitic than his, might be described as soapy.

'As a Bishop,' he said, 'it would ill beseem me to show a want of charity toward any of God's creatures—even toward one whose earthly life was verra far from being a suitable pattern for a Christian King. I am truly sorry that you suppose yourself to have been overlooked by a University in whose founding you played a trifling, purely ceremonial part—'

The King broke in. 'How could I have done more than I did? The University of London was being founded that same year, and of course I had a great deal to do with that. The older universities were offended, so I had to found those readerships in mineralogy and geology at Oxford to appease them. And you know how much I was involved in the Literary Fund, granting them a Charter, and as much money as I could scrape up at the time. I was always short. Generosity—it's a costly indulgence, Bishop. Literature was my real love. Byron—how I admired him; and do you know, for a time at least, he admired me. And noble, generous Walter Scott—a dear friend. I always meant to do something in the way of a Civil List recognition for Jane Austen—dear, ironical Jane, her pretty novels taught me so much about people— even though she was somewhat hard on the clergy. And in all that, I couldn't do much more than I did for little Toronto, now could I? Was it to be expected? Such a busy life, you see.'

The Bishop looked sour, like a man who has been outbid at an auction. 'Busy,' said he; 'aye, busy in the pursuit of pleasure.'

'True, true,' said the King, not in the least daunted. 'I've been called that, you know—the Prince of Pleasure.'

'And where has it brought you?' said the Bishop. 'Think, think man, upon your present unhappy state.'

'What unhappy state?' said the King, much surprised. 'I'm as happy as—well, as happy as a King. I mingle in admirable society, and I don't have to be tedious any more about rank. I can see as much as I please of the literary company I always longed for. Instead—of course it's not proper for ordinary people to kiss and tell, but I *am* a King—dear Jane Austen has been one of my mistresses for the past—oh, well over a century. No great sensation 57 in bed, I assure you, but a wonderful talker; so I talk to Jane and sleep with other ladies whose talent lies that way.'

The Bishop was furious. 'Reprobate!' he, roared, quite forgetting what is due from a Bishop to the Defender of his Faith; 'dare you tell me that you pursue your dissolute courses unrebuked in Hell?'

'Who said anything about Hell?' said the King, much surprised. 'You don't suppose I'm in Hell, do you?'

'If not Hell, where?'

'In Elysium, of course. Where are you?'

'I am in Paradise,' said the Bishop, like a man transformed. 'In Jerusalem, the golden, with milk and honey blessed. Can you believe it, when I arrived, there was not a University, or a good private school, or an Association for the Improvement of Deserving Artisans, or an almshouse for the widows of indigent clergy, or a society for the Relief of Decayed Gentlewomen, or a Society for distributing trusses to the ruptured poor, or a single evidence of practical benevolence in the whole of Paradise? And it has been my glorious care to found them all. And to found many, many more. And there are persons of wealth, to be cajoled and bullied and shamed into giving me the money to do it. Oh, what glorious tussles I've had with some of them! Man, it's Heaven. Work, work, work, and found, found, found, and beg, beg, beg without cease. I

have turned the new Jerusalem into a splendid likeness of

modern Toronto. Oh, the goodness of our bountiful Creator! He has even provided Sin—Sin in unlimited quantity and horrendous quality, for his Blessed Ones like myself to struggle with and combat and overcome. At this present moment I am busy with an area of the New Jerusalem where shameless men resort to have their bodies rubbed by unclothed women. Aye, and there is an abomination quite new since my time, a group called The Gays, and it is my resolve to assail their New Sodom. How can a poor lost soul like yourself judge of the holy ecstasy that Paradise is to a man like me?'

'I'll keep to Elysium,' said the King.

'But you ought to be in Hell,' shouted the Bishop.

'Oh it would be Hell to you, just as your Paradise would be Hell to me,' said the King. 'You'd find Elysium way over your head. The daylight hours are spent in a sort of perpetual banquet, interspersed with expeditions on the water, and there's an opera every evening. And after lights out—no, no, Bishop, not for you. Of course I build a lot of new palaces, and you should see the gardens I'm planning. And furniture! Had it never struck you that a really satisfactory hereafter would involve perpetual delicious anxieties about new furniture? And—this is God's charity at its most thoughtful—nobody ever sends in a bill!'

The Bishop's face was an arena in which Pity wrestled 59

with Outraged Virtue. 'Man, man,' he said, 'do ye never tire of pleasure?'

'Tire—of pleasure? What an extraordinary idea. Do you ever tire of good works?'

'Never! But good works, inspired by faith—'

'What kind of faith? Do you make nothing of my life-long faith in art and beauty? I wasn't an artist myself—except perhaps in my personal appearance—but I was a great patron, a great appreciator and inspirer, a commissioner of fine things, and a notable collector. Do you call that nothing?'

'I call it self-indulgence.'

'You, my lord, are a savage.'

'Do you call me a savage, you crowned and anointed buffoon! You jewelled and gilded puppet, good for nothing but silly folk to gape at!'

'Very well. I withdraw "savage"; it was an unworthy name for a King to apply to a Bishop of his own Church. But I shall say this; you are not a gentlephantom.'

'The rank is but the guinea stamp. I was one of the World's Workers.'

'Then we shall never agree. You were devoted to what Davies here'—the King nodded toward me—'would doubtless call the Work Ethic. Whereas I was devoted to the Pleasure Principle. I enjoyed life and I encouraged enjoyment in others. On balance I think my kind of person has done rather more for mankind than yours.'

But John Strachan was not to be talked down. 'Upon what is a University built if not upon the Work Ethic? What has the scholar to offer to his God greater than Work and Prayer?'

'What would God make of a university filled with nothing but sweaty psalm-singers?' said the King. 'God, as a gentleman and an Anglican, must certainly appreciate scholarship, intellectual dignity, connoisseurship—all the attributes of civilization, and civilization owes more to the Pleasure Principle than it does to the Work Ethic, which is moneygrubbing humbug. That was why I took pains to put a representative of the Pleasure Principle in this University at its beginning. Yes, right under your nose, my careful friend, and you never saw what I had done.'

'And what was that?' The Bishop's voice was scornful and suspicious.

'It wasn't a that; it was a who,' said the King.

'Who, then?'

'A member of my family.'

'Hut! There was no member of your family here at the founding.'

'Oh, but there was. Surely you remember him? Indeed you yourself appointed him. Have you forgotten the Reverend John McCaul, first professor of Classics, and successor to yourself as President of the University?'

'John McCaul; a man of God; a man after my own heart!'

'Perhaps. But also my nephew.'

It is impossible for a ghost to have a seizure of apoplexy, but certainly that was what the ghost of Bishop Strachan seemed to be suffering. As he fought for breath, the King continued triumphantly.

'Surely you remember, my lord, that John McCaul came to Canada under the direct patronage of the Archbishop of Canterbury? My brothers were a wild lot of fellows, and they had many sons on the wrong side of the blanket. Like any good English family, we followed the custom of the day: convicts to Australia—bastards to Canada. John McCaul was of the Blood Royal.'

With a might effort, the Bishop raised his hand, and, like a meteor, a volume of the *Dictionary of National Biography* emerged from one of the arrow-slits in the Robarts Library and sailed down into his outstretched hand, open at page 446 of Volume XII. The King and I read therein an entry describing the somewhat unremarkable life of one Alexander McCaul, and Irish scholar and divine, which concluded with the curt entry: 'He left several sons.'

'Aha,' said the King, 'you observe that this very Victorian compilation says nothing whatever about the good parson's wife. But she was well-known in her day. Well-known to my brother Fred, among others. Young John was his lad. You must have heard the rumours?'

The Bishop was shielding his eyes with his hand, but he shook his head.

Now it was the King's turn. He lifted his hand and at once came the response from Robarts—a volume bound in red which I had no trouble in recognizing as *University College—a Portrait*, edited by Claude T. Bissell. There, on pages 4 and 5, the Bishop and I read: "The Reverend John McCaul remained Professor of Classics, and became President of the University of Toronto. He had come to Canada in 1839 as Principal of Upper Canada College, on the special recommendation of the Archbishop of Canterbury; and this fact, as well as *certain rumours as to his royal parentage* explain perhaps his preferment in Canada, and his survival of forty years of bitter controversy over university affairs".

'There, you see,' said the King. 'It was obvious to anybody who looked at him; obvious still, if you take a good look at the portrait of young Jack in the Great Hall of Hart House. He's the spitting image of my brother Augustus Frederick, Duke of Sussex. Fred was always fond of classics, so the lad came by it honestly. Fred asked the Archbishop to find something for young Jack, and of course he did.'

It seemed to me that the King had won, hands down, and I thought it a little ungenerous of him to dance upon the body of a fallen foe.

'Come along, Dr. Strachan, we must return our books 63

to the Library; others may want them, you know.' He tossed the history of University College into the air, and like a swallow it sped back to Robarts; the Bishop's book was slower to return than it had been in coming, and laboured in its flight, like a turkey. The King continued to rub salt into the wound.

'I think it rather shabby of the University to have grudged John McCaul some recognition of his royal parentage. I want you to take care of that, Davies. In this Sesquicentennial year, you must have—well, not the royal arms, but the arms of the Duke of Sussex affixed to the top of the frame of his picture. With a proper attaint of bastardy on it, of course. It would do a little something to make up for the University's shabby treatment of me.'

Bishop Strachan's face was still buried in his hands, but his voice, choked with tears, could be heard. 'Och, Johnnie McCaul, could ye no have confided your shame to your Bishop?' he sobbed.

'Oh don't be such an old Goosey Gander, Strachan,' said the King. 'McCaul's bastardy was his glory, and reflected glory on this University. Consider the Pleasure Principle and dry your eyes. You look a perfect quiz. And be realistic Strachan (His Majesty insisted on giving full, phlegmy Scottish honours to the name)—how do you expect anyone to survive as a University President who is not, in one sense or another, a bastard? Now Davies, I rely on you; have that heraldic ornament on young Jack's frame before the Sesquicentennial Year ends.'

Here was a pretty kettle of fish! But I remembered something Vincent Massey had told me, years ago.

'Your Majesty is by no means forgotten in this University,' said I. 'Have you visited the Senate Chamber?'

'Should I?'

'If you would be so gracious as to do so,' said I, 'you would see that above the Chancellor's great chair in that handsome room there is a splendid achievement of arms. You would immediately recognize them, Sire, for they are your own. And they were placed there by the designer of that room, who was also the Founder of this College.'

'Damme, that was handsomely done of Vincent Massey,' said the King. 'I knew there was some reason why I came to weep in Massey College. An understanding spirit, that's what I discerned here.'

'Mr. Massey told me it was not managed without some dispute,' said I. 'The late Canon Cody, who was President at that time, was strongly against it; he objected that you were a bad example to Canadian youth. But in the end Mr. Massey prevailed. So you see, the Pleasure Principle is symbolized at the very heart of the University.'

'And can do it nothing but good,' said the King, beaming. Then he drew a splendid watch from his pocket. 'I must be going,' said he, 'if I am to be in time to hear *The Magic Flute;* little Mozart is conducting it himself. Fare- 65 well for the present, Davies; and you might just as well get on with that job on McCaul's portrait. Hope to see you in Elysium.'

'But not too soon,' I murmured, bowing as the King melted into the night air. I turned to take leave of Bishop Strachan, but he had gone already. Where he had stood were several little holes in the path, where his bitter tears had eaten into the stone.

The Ugly Spectre of Sexism

At the College dance last week a young man, a former member of this College, approached me and screamed—in order to be heard above the music—'Are you going to have a Ghost Story for us this year?' I screamed back, 'I really don't know.' 'Oh yes you do,' he shrieked; 'I'll bet you've got it tucked away in a drawer right this minute.' Then he went to the bar to take something for his throat. Because, as those of you who attend modern dances understand, a conversation of that length, conducted while the band is giving its all, is a considerable strain on the vocal cords.

He had put his finger on a sore spot in my mind. I had no Ghost Story, and my dilemma was an ugly one: on the one hand I didn't want to disappoint you, and on the other I shrank from meeting any more College ghosts, because it is always an exhausting, and sometimes a humiliating experience.

After all, this College is well advanced in its eleventh year, and we have had a ghost story every Christmas. Ten ghosts, surely, is enough for any college? In a modern building, such a superfluity of ghosts is almost a reflection on the contractors. Or could it, on the other hand, be some metaphysical emanation from the spirit of the Founders who were, to a man, connoisseurs of *bizarrerie?* Or—and this, I assure you, is where the canker gnaws—is there something about me that attracts such manifestations? There are men who attract dogs. There are men of a very different kind who attract women. Can it be that I attract ghosts?

Pondering thus, I wandered out into the quad, where the music was somewhat less oppressive. Yet, even in the chill air I felt myself a prey to melancholy apprehension. What was it about that music that made it so disturbing? It seemed as if it were the spirit of our time, made manifest in sound. Loud, compelling, insistent yet turbulent; rhythmic, but always threatening to break the bounds of rhythm and rage into some new and fiercely evocative mode. This was music that seemed to be imploring the gods to answer in all the primal, untrammelled majesty of a storm.

The noise mounted to a climax and I heard cheers from within. The moment had come for which modern dancers wait in worshipping expectation; the percussion man was going to perform a solo. The banging, crashing and rattling he produced was sheer sound, unhampered by any suggestion of a tune or a tone. It was heaven-storming music, and I felt myself yielding to it. My nerves were fiercely alert.

As I walked toward the College gate my glance rose,

and at once I knew that something was amiss. Or, rather, was missing. Where was the great bull's head which normally presides over the exit from the Quad? Not in its place? Impossible. It must be a delusion caused by the excellent supper at the dance. But—where was the Bull? 'Bah! Humbug!' I said to myself as I stood looking out into Devonshire Place. The December wind that had been sweeping through it grew, in a matter of seconds, into a whirlwind. Dust, twigs, debris of all sorts was whirling in this tempest; some of it swept toward me and I became aware that a mass of newspaper was dashing itself against the gate, and might well blow through it. I like the quad to be tidy, and I pushed it away with my foot. To my amazement, it resisted, with a power that wind alone could not explain. I kicked at it and—how am I to tell you?—it seemed to give a cry, in an almost human voice. The sound of the percussion solo from the Hall became more demanding in its intensity, and I lost my self-possession. I kicked and pushed at the mass of newspaper with hands and feet, and the more I fought the fiercer it became, until at last it forced itself through the bars of the gate, and stood—yes, stood!—before me.

'Thing of evil,' I cried—and even as I spoke I knew that I had once again slipped into the rhetorical manner of speech which these spectres always impose upon me— 'Thing of evil, what would you here? Whence, and what are you?'

The mass of newspaper appeared to be winded by our struggle, and its reply, though audible, was incomprehensible to me. But the tone was unmistakably that of a woman's voice.

'Speak up!' I demanded.

The mass of newspaper raised one of its outlying rags of newsprint and pointed toward what would have been, in a human figure, its head.

I leaned down for a closer look, because the figure was considerably shorter than I. At its top, which was twirled up into a sort of point, I was able to make out *Toronto Star, February 1, 1972.*

'You are the *Toronto Star?*' said I, half in fear, half in derision, as academics usually speak when they are dealing with newspapers.

The figure nodded its head, then pointed with what seemed to be its Homemakers' Section toward a headline which was at the place where, if it had indeed been a woman, its bosom would have been found. I put on my reading spectacles and peeped delicately at its bosom. The words there were familiar and made me recoil. They read: *The Ugly Spectre of Sexism Lurks at Massey College.*

I remembered that headline. It was on February 1, 1972, that the *Toronto Star* had printed a letter from a young woman who was aggrieved by what she considered the indefensible discrimination of this College against her sex. Not only was this place manifestly elitist, she said,

70

but it was sexist as well, and in the modern world, this was not to be endured. I looked at the bundle of newspaper again; there was something feminine about its general outline, certainly, but what was it, and what did it mean?

'Frankly, you don't look like *The Star*—' I began. But the creature had found its voice and burst out in an excited squeak.

'None of that!' it said. 'I know you sexists. Next thing you'll be telling me I'm too pretty to be a great national daily. I've come to do a colour story on the Ugly Spectre of Sexism that lurks at Massey College. Where do your spectres usually lurk? Point the way and then leave me alone, you old sexist.'

'I resent being called a sexist,' I said, with dignity. 'But you are a guest here, and I shall treat you with courtesy regardless of your rudeness to me. We have no spectres but I shall gladly offer you some spirits. I could do with a double Scotch, myself.'

'That'll be fine,' said the strange visitor, in a somewhat mollified tone. I was about to go to the bar for drinks, but something happened that made it clear that however ragged and rubbishy its appearance, I was in the presence of a supernatural being, and that the atmosphere was strangely fraught. Suddenly, from nowhere, two double Scotches were hovering in the air before us, and I gestured to my companion to accept one. She immediately proved that, ghost or not, she belonged to the newspaper world by taking that which my practised eye told me was slightly the bigger. After a hearty swig had disappeared into the folds of newspaper my strange companion spoke again, in a tone that betrayed a little self-doubt.

'This *is* Massey College?' it squeaked.

'You mean you're not sure?' said I.

'The editor wouldn't give me money for a taxi,' it said, 'so I came on the wind and I've had a rough journey. That's why I'm late.'

'Late for what?' I said.

'For striking terror and dismay into your black heart,' said the creature. 'Because you discriminate against women. Because you are a barnacle on the Ship of Progress. Because you are a miserable Neo-Piscean who is trying to halt the approach of the Age of Aquarius. Because you are a fascist-recidivist-elitist-chauvinist-pig. I am here to expose you. Then your nerve will break and the Junior Fellows will throw open the gates to women and hail a new dawn.'

'You are even later than you think,' said I. 'The new dawn of which you speak was hailed on May 11 of this year when it was decided by our senior fascist-recidivist-elitist-chauvinist-pigs, meeting in solemn council, and with the full concurrence of those of our Founders who are still living, that women should be admitted to this college under the same conditions as men, beginning next September.'

72

'Aha! So we drove you to it,' said the figure.

'Not in the least,' said I. 'This college follows a star, but not the Toronto *Star*. You are too late.'

The figure seemed to lose height. 'You mean there's no Ugly Spectre of Sexism,' it said, in a wistful, papery voice. I felt sorry for the frail little creature.

'Why don't you just take a quick look around, and then go back and say you didn't find anything and it isn't worth bothering about?' I said.

Once again the figure became shrill. 'None of your helpful suggestions,' it squeaked; 'none of your masculine gallantry toward the defeated female. I'm onto your game; you want to disarm me with kindness, but you won't do it!'

'I must say you're very hard to please,' said I. 'And I can't go on arguing with you unless I can call you something. What's your name?'

'You'd better call me Ms.' said the figure.

'To me Ms. has always meant Manuscript,' I said, 'and you're not Manuscript, or even Typescript. You're that most dismal form of letterpress, an out-of-date newspaper. I think I'll call you Scrap, because you're scrap paper and because you're so scrappy.'

To my surprise Scrap giggled. 'Now you're talking like a fellow-creature,' she said. 'How about another Scotch?'

Hardly had I formed the thought than two glasses were in the air between us, and again Scrap grabbed the larger. 73

I thought I saw a rude twinkle where her eye should have been. 'Here's my hand up your gown, Master,' Scrap said.

I am not to be outdone in colloquialism. 'Here's thumbing through your Index,' said I. We drank. It was very good whisky, which is not perhaps surprising, as it obviously came from the spirit world. After her second drink Scrap was quite friendly.

'I think I'll take you up on that offer of a look around,' said she. I shall refer to her henceforward as 'she' because the more Scrap drank the more feminine she became. 'Want to come?'

I nodded. But I was concerned. Where was our Bull?

'Mind you, it has to be understood that you're following,' said Scrap. 'There's to be none of this chauvinist-pig nonsense of showing the little lady over the place. I don't need a guide.'

So off we went. We started with the carrel area, and Scrap was in a perfect ecstasy, dodging in and out among the partitions, disguising herself as the contents of a waste-paper basket, and popping out at me from what she hoped were unexpected places, with cheerful squeaks of 'Boo!' It was rather like going for a walk with a mischievous dog. But as she dashed ahead of me I noticed that for all her Women's Lib principles she was uncommonly feminine, and now and then, when she was out of sight, I heard that sound which had such a stimulating effect on our Victorian forefathers—the delicate rustle of skirts. It was clear that Scrap was not wanting in feminine arts, and if I had been younger, and not a philosopher, I suppose I would have ended up chasing her.

She was delighted with the Chapel, and twitched aside the curtains behind the altar, as a likely place for the Ugly Spectre of Sexism to be lurking. She took a long look at our altar-piece, and said: 'Who's this woman, painted inside a star?' 'That is a depiction of Divine Wisdom, always represented as woman,' said I.

'Right on!' said Scrap, approvingly.

Then we climbed the stairs, and came to the door of the Round Room. This will stop her, I thought; a spectre might lurk in a place that is full of corners, but to lurk within a circle is an impossibility. And that shows how much I knew about it. Pride came before my fall.

As we entered the Round Room the sense of being haunted descended upon me like a mist. The room was lit by an eerie, flickering blue light, which moved and stirred so restlessly that for a few seconds I could see nothing clearly. Therefore I was startled when a deep, authoritative voice, which was certainly not that of Scrap, said: 'You're late. Just like a woman. I've been expecting you. Sit down.'

The speaker was a figure so astonishing and alarming that for a moment I thought that I might swoon. He—certainly it was a he—was tall of figure, huge of chest, slim of flank, and wore elegant evening dress. Not a dinner jacket, which is often seen here; a white tie, and a tail coat of the most distinguished tailoring. But it was his head that struck awe and terror into my heart. It was huge, and it was the head of a bull. And no common bull either, but the Bull from over our gate, and from its left ear hung a massive ornament of jet, within which a fleur-de-lis was outlined in diamonds.

'The Massey Bull,' I shrieked.

'Obviously,' said the creature.

Scrap was dancing so wildly that she seemed to blow about the room on a breeze. 'You said I wouldn't find him, and I have! It's the Ugly Spectre of Sexism that lurks at Massey College!'

An expression passed over the face of the creature which I shall not attempt to describe, but it was enough to cause Scrap to crumple away in alarm. 'I am the heraldic bull of Massey College,' it said, with great dignity. 'I am, in a special and exalted sense, the totem-animal of this academic, all-male community. I stand, very properly, at the top of its coat-of-arms, and over its entrance. I am, as you may see, unmistakably masculine. I scorn to lurk. I pervade. And I demand to know what you, Master, and presumably this bundle of wastepaper here, mean by proposing to admit women under what I regard, with unchallenged right, as my roof?'

What was I to say? Fortunately I didn't have to say anything, because Scrap began to whirl in the air around the creature, squeaking: 'Admit women, did you say? Just you try to keep them out! You'll have me to reckon with. I'm Ms. let me tell you, and here I stay till this place is full of women. I'm going to make you all miserable till you acknowledge that the day of masculine supremacy is over, and you'd better get that through your big hairy head. Masculine indeed! You earring-wearer! The day of barnyard rule and barnyard ethics is done, and the glorious pennon of Unisex is being unfurled over every bastion of masculine privilege in the civilized world!'

The bull lowered his great head and fixed Ms. with red eyes. He blew a snorting breath from his nostrils that could only mean trouble. I felt that I should say something, and as I didn't know what to say of course I said something foolish.

'Surely you young people can find some grounds of compromise,' said I. They both turned on me with such anger that I feared they would attack me. To be manhandled is unpleasant, but it is a far more dreadful thing to be ghost-handled; one's metabolism is never the same afterward.

'You sit down,' said the Bull; 'We are going to debate this matter, Ms. and I, of the admission of women to Massey College. You shall be referee,' he said, and with a sharp side-wise hook of his dexter horn he tossed me into the red chair in which it is humorously supposed I preside in that room. There was nothing for it but to obey.

'Ladies first,' said I, nodding toward Scrap.

She was furious. 'There you go,' she squeaked, 'hoping to disarm me with old-world courtesy. I won't go first. You won't get a word out of me.' But then she rushed onward with an extraordinary torrent of speech in which I could only catch a few phrases like 'minority group antagonism,' 'insensitive to cultural mood,' 'oppression as an institutionalized social function,' 'dynamics of victimization,' and the like. Coming from one who was supposed not to be speaking at all it took rather a long time, and the Bull grew impatient, pawed the ground and tossed his great head. At last he was so angry that flame—yes, flame—burst from his nostrils. Scrap, so highly inflammable, was in serious danger.

Seemingly, she knew no fear. If I had not seen it with my own eyes I would not have believed what happened next. Scrap, with a furious gesture, tore from the area of her bosom a strip of newsprint, and held it in the flame, in which it was immediately consumed. But not before I saw what was printed on it. It was a lingerie advertisement, and it bore a nicely drawn depiction of a brassiere.

'Defiance!' she shrieked. 'That is the ultimate act of feminine defiance! Match it, if you can!'

The Bull laughed a deep taurine laugh. 'Typical feminine argument,' said he; 'you refuse to be considered as a sexual object, and yet you underline your refusal with a flagrantly sexual gesture. Is that your muddle-headed way of saying that you place no value on your sex?'

'I'll tell you what the value of my sex is,' snarled Scrap. 'It's value has been established by Xaviera Hollander, the Happy Hooker herself, and it's five hundred dollars a shot.'

I was dismayed by this indelicacy, and the ease with which she had fallen into the trap. The Bull sneered. He drew a paper from his breast pocket and laid it on the desk in front of me. 'I offer this as evidence in contradiction,' said he; 'this is the present male rate.' I looked at the card and blenched. It contained some intimate information about the erotic tariff of the celebrated race-horse Secretariat. I must say it made Xaviera Hollander look like cheap goods. But my sense of propriety was outraged.

'I refuse to listen to argument on this coarse level,' said I. 'Whatever arrangements you two wish to make in privacy, as Consenting Spectres, is nobody's business but your own, but I will have no part in it. This argument must continue, if at all, on a level of decency.'

'Very well,' said the Bull. 'Allow me to remind everyone present that only a month ago a Princess of the Realm, surely an example to all young women, took a public vow to OBEY the man who became her husband. And several young men in this College got up at five o'clock in the morning to hear her do it.'

This time it was Scrap who laughed, and it was immediately clear that laughter was something the Bull had not expected. He glared angrily, but he was confused, and Scrap took shrewd advantage of his confusion.

'Are you so besotted with male vanity you don't know what the Princess had in mind?' said she. 'Must I show you what feminine obedience means?'

From the mass of paper of which she was composed, Scrap produced a sheet printed entirely in red, and she began to trail it, slowly and provocatively in front of the Bull. I could hardly believe what followed. As if hypnotised, its great head began to roll to left and right, as it followed this transfixing red cloak, which gave out the characteristic feminine rustle that I had noticed before.

'Let's see who does the obeying now,' whispered Scrap.

O for the pen of an Ernest Hemingway, that I might adequately describe for you the spectacle of art and brutality that followed! Scrap was all femininity as she glided, not rapidly but with splendid grace, around the ring of our Round Room. As she moved she murmured in a low, compelling, unbearably taunting voice, 'Ah, toro, toro! Here—here to me, toro! Aha! Toro! Toro!' And the Bull, unable to help himself, responded to every word and gesture.

Do you know our Round Room? There are twenty-two
80 tall black chairs in it, and on the back of every chair is

stamped, in gold, the head of a bull. As Scrap led her victim in his fated dance, I saw that the forty-four eyes of those bulls followed every move: their forty-four nostrils stirred with growing apprehension, and I thought I saw the frothy spittle of fear dripping from their twenty-two tongues.

What was I to do? Where did my sympathies lie? I was, if you will pardon the bluntness of my speech, a quivering ganglion of irreconcilable emotions. I ought to stop the fight. I ought to help the Bull, who was as surely doomed as any bull I have ever seen in a ring. But the skill shown by Scrap thrilled me. Without knowing how it happened, I found myself standing on my desk cheering. I even snatched the rose from my buttonhole and threw it into the ring.

The fight did not last long, but it was splendid while it lasted. More and more furiously the Bull responded to the taunts of Scrap, whose elegance as a matador was beautiful to behold. Her *veronicas*, her *amontillados*, her *tournedos bonne femme* were as fine as anything I have ever seen, in the great *corridas* of Madrid. But all the time I wondered: How is she going to finish him off? She has no weapon, except that which she had pretended to hold in contempt—her feminine fascination, her charm.

As I have said, the light was ghost-light, and I have but

mortal eyes. Suddenly there was a crash and the Bull was down; he had stepped on the rose I had thrown, slipped, and cracked his great head on the corner of one of our curved tables. I was cheering wildly.

But to my astonishment, Scrap was weeping. She stumbled blindly about the Round Room, looking for a corner in which to hide her head; on the floor lay the Bull, apparently dead. I thought he looked rather noble in death—until he winked at me. I had no time for reflection, because Scrap was pulling at my sleeve.

'Call me a trash-bin,' she sobbed, 'and let me get away from here.'

'But you've won,' said I. 'I presume you mean to take over the College. Isn't that what all this is about?'

'I didn't mean to kill him,' sobbed Scrap. 'I only meant to teach him a lesson. What shall I do without him?'

There are certain advantages in being no longer young. One sees a little more clearly, even without one's glasses. 'Leave everything to me,' said I. 'And you really mustn't go away. I think you'll like it here. And I think we're going to like you. Now let me put you in a nice restful place to think it all over until next September.'

And, with gallantry which Scrap did not now refuse, I gave her my arm and led her through the labyrinths of the lower part of the College, and there I put her in a very comfortable part of the Library to rest. I took care that she did not see what was printed on the door behind which I locked her, but I don't mind telling you. It said *Printed Ephemera*.

Then I hastened back to the Round Room to render first aid to the Bull. I knew that he had simply knocked his head against a reality but I thought his self-esteem might need some delicate attention.

He had gone. The Ugly Spectre of Sexism was lurking at Massey College no longer. And as I walked out into the quad I saw that he was back in his accustomed place over the gate, and I noticed, as you may notice if you choose, that, noble as he looks, and invincible as he looks, he has an undoubted black eye. But with his right eye he winked again. And I observed that he was wearing his huge single ear-ring with a new jauntiness as though he had discovered, in his brief encounter with Scrap, the truth that in the most redoubtably masculine creature there lurks some strain of the feminine.

All seemed peace in the College as I walked again in the quad. Even the music from the dance was peaceful, for the band was playing a Golden Oldie, *You're the Cream in my Coffee:*

> You will always be
> My necessity
> Can't get along without you—

I hummed, and winked back at the Bull.

The great clock of Hart House struck a single resonant note. Everybody in the University knows what that sound means. 'Great Heaven,' I cried, 'it must be two o'clock.' And I hurried back to the dance.

FOR THE BEST IN PAPERBACKS, LOOK FOR THE 🐧

In every corner of the world, on every subject under the sun, Penguin represents quality and variety—the very best in publishing today.

For complete information about books available from Penguin—including Puffins, Penguin Classics, and Arkana—and how to order them, write to us at the appropriate address below. Please note that for copyright reasons the selection of books varies from country to country.

In the United States: Please write to *Consumer Sales, Penguin USA, P.O. Box 999, Dept. 17109, Bergenfield, New Jersey 07621-0120.* Visa and MasterCard holders call 1-800-253-6476 to order all Penguin titles.

In Canada: Please write to *Penguin Books Canada Ltd, 10 Alcorn Avenue, Suite 300, Toronto, Ontario M4V 3B2.*

In the United Kingdom: Please write to *Dept. JC, Penguin Books Ltd, FREEPOST, West Drayton, Middlesex UB7 OBR.*